The Fabulous World of Mr. Fred

To life-changing encounters. —L. C.

To a great friend, Ève Léveillée, for everything... —G. G.

5 4 3 2 1

Published in Canada by Fitzhenry & Whiteside, 195 Allstate Parkway, Markham, ON, L3R 4T8
www.fitzhenry.ca
Published in the U.S. by Fitzhenry & Whiteside, 311 Washington Street, Brighton, Massachusetts 02135
Originally published in 2012 as Le monde fabuleux de M. Fred by Dominique et compagnie Quebec, a division of Editions Heritage Inc., Quebec, Canada, J4R 1 K5.

We acknowledge with thanks the Canada Council for the Arts, and the Ontario Arts Council for their support of our publishing program. We acknowledge the financial support of the Government of Canada through the Canada Book Fund (CBF) for our publishing activities.

Canada Council for the Arts
Conseil des Arts du Canada

Library and Archives Canada Cataloguing in Publication
The Fabulous World of Mr. Fred
ISBN 978-1-55455-346-4 (paperback)
Data available on file

Publisher Cataloging-in-Publication Data (U.S.)
The Fabulous World of Mr. Fred
ISBN 978-1-55455-346-4 (paperback)
Data available on file

Text and cover design by Daniel Choi
Cover illustration courtesy of Gabrielle Grimard

Printed and bound in China by Sheck Wah Tong Printing Press Ltd.

The Fabulous World of Mr. Fred

Lili Chartrand

Illustrated by Gabrielle Grimard

Fitzhenry & Whiteside

My name is Pierrot.

Growing up, I always had my head in the clouds.

I daydreamed so often that many people thought I was crazy! All my friends were imaginary, until the day I met Mr. Fred…

After school one day, for no particular reason, I decided to cross the park to get home.

Suddenly, I was drawn to a man sitting on a bench. Head bent, he was turning the pages of a book—an *invisible* book.

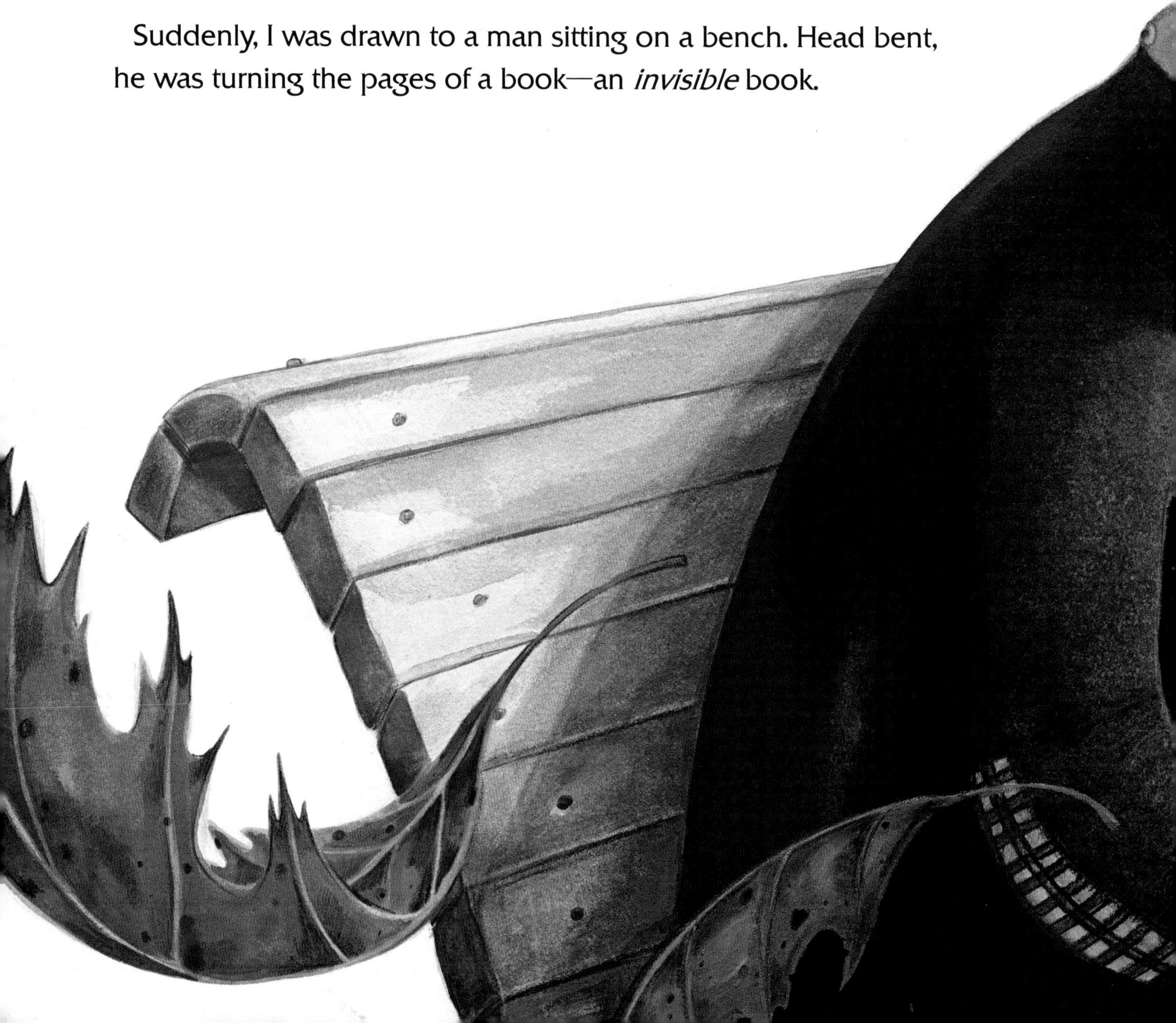

Curious, I sat beside the man.

"Your book looks quite interesting! What's it about?"

"It's a collection of stories," the man replied, his little, bright eyes settling onto mine. "If you'd like, I could read you one."

I nodded my head quickly. I loved stories!

He asked me my name and I asked him his.

"My name is Mr. Fred."

Mr. Fred read while turning the invisible pages. It was magical! When the magnificent story was over, he looked tired.

I thanked him and stood up.

He said to me, "If you'd like, we can meet again tomorrow afternoon."

I was thrilled.

The next day, on the same bench, Mr. Fred
was flipping through his invisible book.

We smiled at each other
and I took a seat next to him.

His eyes shining bright, Mr. Fred suggested
a story called, "The Broken-Hearted Tree."

When the story was over, I exclaimed,
"I love that story. It's brilliant!"

Mr. Fred was so delighted,
he looked ten years younger!

We shook hands and parted.
I couldn't wait for our next meeting.

When I arrived at the park the next day, I pleaded with Mr. Fred to re-read the story of the tree. I had dreamt about it all night!

He stared at me for a long time and tears appeared in his eyes.

"You remind me so much of my son! It was his favourite story, too. It begins on page 46," he said before he began reading.

It was such a fascinating story! I was so excited that I asked Mr. Fred to read me another story.

After a moment of silence, Mr. Fred said, "I'd like to tell you the story of my life instead."

I held my breath.

"I was a boy filled with dreams," Mr. Fred began. "Over the years, many of those dreams came true. But three years ago, I almost died in a house fire. I lost my wife, my son and my two cats. I thought I would go insane. For a long time, I lived on the streets."

I was speechless.

Mr. Fred continued, “But, sometimes, it is in the darkness that light shines. My lucky star is named Mrs. Sweetpea. She reached out to me a year ago. I’ve lived in her attic ever since. I sweep her entrance, take our her trash, mow her lawn and do her shopping. In return, I am fed and have a roof over my head.”

I watched him. He was younger than he appeared, but he seemed as fragile as glass.

"Meeting you has done me a world of good," Mr. Fred admitted to me.

I blushed. No one had ever said such kind words to me.

"You introduced yourself to me and didn't treat me like I was crazy," he added. "Like my son, you believe in the impossible. I also used to read him this book…I thought of reading it again because I was feeling lonely. I'm so glad I did because it brought me a wonderful new friend."

My heart leapt with joy.

I finally had a real friend, and what a great friend he was!

I was so happy I jumped up and hugged him.

Mr. Fred muffled a cry of surprise.

I excused myself. He laughed a little and hugged me back.

The next day, after school, I headed out with my head down toward the park. I was so excited by this new friendship that during recess, I told everyone about Mr. Fred and his invisible book.

All the children laughed at me, chanting, "Crazy Pierrot! Crazy Pierrot!"

Everyone, that is, except for the new girl, Lila, who looked at me without saying a word.

To make matters worse, Mr. Fred wasn't at the park.

I asked a shopkeeper if he knew Mrs. Sweetpea.

"Certainly! She lives in that small, blue house over there," he said, pointing at the house.

Two minutes later, I found myself in front of an old, hunched lady who was sweeping her entrance. I introduced myself and asked about Mr. Fred.

"I hope he isn't sick…"

"My poor child! Mr. Fred has been suffering for a long time now. He passed away this morning."

My heart was tight. I couldn't speak.

I'd lost my only true friend.

"He left this package for you, though," she said.

With the package under my arm, I ran to the park. Sitting on our bench, I felt sad and curious at the same time. I tore open the envelope.

It contained a manuscript. On the cover, a small message was inscribed with a shaky hand.

Dear Pierrot,
I leave you my treasure.
With all my love,
Mr. Fred

I flipped through the pages. They were his stories! Immediately, I searched for page 46, for the story of "The Broken-Hearted Tree." Mr. Fred had written down all the stories that he had invented for his son…He knew them by heart!

And I, Crazy Pierrot, had inherited his precious treasure.

I began reading "The Broken-Hearted Tree" right away.

The story reminded me so much of my friendship with Mr. Fred. Lost in the story, I jumped when a small voice asked me, "What are you reading?"

It was Lila.

I invited her to sit next to me and I finished reading the rest of the story.

Her green eyes filled with wonder and I decided to share my treasure with her. I read aloud all the stories. Lila was enchanted. So was I.

That day, we became friends.

Twenty years passed. I married Lila and we had a son.

His name is Freddie. We live in Mrs. Sweetpea's house.

The attic is my favourite spot to read Mr. Fred's stories to my son. His collection was published and his treasure is now shared with thousands of children.